Bobby Brewster's typewriter

Through his appearances on television, and the story-telling sessions he has held in libraries, schools and at parties in Australia, New Zealand and South Africa as well as in almost every part of Britain, H. E. Todd can claim to be the best known story-teller in the world.

Here are eight stories about his favourite character, Bobby Brewster, the boy to whom the most extraordinary things happen.

D1337492

H. E. TODD

Bobby Brewster's typewriter

Illustrated by Lilian Buchanan

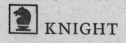 KNIGHT

in association with SCHOLASTIC PUBLICATIONS

ISBN 0 340 17359 9

This edition first published 1973 by Knight, the paperback
division of Brockhampton Press, Leicester.

First published in 1971 by Brockhampton Press Ltd

Text copyright © 1971 H. E. Todd
Illustrations copyright © 1971 Brockhampton Press Ltd

Printed and bound in Great Britain by Cox & Wyman Ltd,
London, Reading and Fakenham

Contents

Introduction

Here is another book of Bobby Brewster's adventures, and what extraordinary adventures they continue to be! Some of them have been written as a result of seeing things – a friend of mine really *has* a cat that is fascinated by her typewriter for instance – and I myself once really *did* see a stocking on a clothes-line give the tail of a shirt a huge kick! I can't honestly say they I heard the shirt cry 'Oh!', but I'm sure it must have done.

Other stories have been written as a result of interesting letters sent by friends after school visits, and their names are quoted below, with my thanks. Most of the stories are merely light-hearted adventures – and why not? – but if you read *What is a weed?* and *The statue* carefully, you might find that there is something more than just amusement in them. Anyway, I hope you enjoy the stories in the book.

My 'Thank yous' are for Stuart Allan, Fiona Baird, Patrick Butcher, Thomas Doughty, Susan Dray, Linda Fyall, Paul Greenstreet, Steven Hall, Rhona Homfray, Jacqueline Langridge, Maura Larmour, Karen Littler,

Clive Murray, Christine Porter, William Ritchie, Maureen Slater, Andrew Taylor, Paul Wooster and many friends at Anlaby Primary School and Horstead Primary School who helped with developing the stories *With knobs on* and *Clothes on the line*.

H. E. TODD

The typewriter

Bobby Brewster has always been fascinated by his father's typewriter. The noise the keys make, the way the letters pop up on to the paper, the tinkle of the bell at the end of each line – there is a certain magic about it. When he was younger he sometimes sat and watched his father typing letters, and was even allowed to tap one or two of the keys himself, but never when he was alone. He promised his father he would not touch that typewriter without permission, and he always kept his promise because he knew how awkward it was when the typewriter went wrong. Last year, when it went away for an overhaul, his father had to write some letters in longhand, and some of them took far too long to reach their destination because the postmen couldn't read his father's writing. And if you could see his father's writing you would understand why. It really is very difficult to read. Even Mr Brewster himself finds it difficult.

Bobby's handwriting isn't all that good either, particularly when he is excited about a story he is writing and is in too much of a hurry. Last term, he handed in a story to Mr Limcano at school, and it came back with the following comment: 'I expect this is a good story, but I am not sure because I can't read it.' Not that Mr Limcano can talk. On Bobby's latest school report he wrote a remark that Mr and Mrs Brewster couldn't read, and they had to ask Mr Limcano to explain what it was. And do you know what he had written so indistinctly on Bobby's report? 'His handwriting is abominable.'

But nowadays some of Bobby's work is much tidier. Do you know why? Because Mr Brewster Senior – that's his grandfather – has given him a small typewriter of his very own. Nothing very elaborate or expensive, but it works and Bobby uses it regularly. Of course, he isn't allowed to take it to school, but Mr Limcano is quite relieved when he types the stories with it at home because they are much easier to mark.

Bobby himself isn't the only one who is fascinated by typewriters. Peeper, the Brewsters' cat, is always there when Bobby types. She sits on the table beside him and watches entranced as the paper is tapped from left to right. Then, when the carriage reaches nearer, she sometimes puts out a paw to catch it. She has even been known to tear the paper with her claws which was very annoying, because on that occasion Bobby was nearly at the end of a sheet and had to re-type it.

Even if she is out in the garden, Peeper somehow seems to sense that Bobby has started typing and in no time she is outside the window clamouring to come in. And when Peeper clamours, she doesn't do it in 'Miaows' but in 'Peeps' which are quite impossible to ignore and very appealing. So Bobby has to open the window and let her in.

Now this happened so often that Bobby began to wonder whether Peeper was learning to type herself. He soon had his answer to that question, because one day last term a very funny thing happened.

Mr Limcano asked the children in the class to

write an essay during the weekend about something in the house. As a special encouragement, because they were doing it for him in their spare time, he offered a prize for the best essay. He didn't tell them what the prize would be. He said he would decide that after he had read the essays.

Usually Bobby quite enjoys composing essays, but that weekend he found it very heavy going. For one thing, he couldn't decide what to write about. He just sat at his typewriter and dithered and changed his mind. Then he started doodling and typing silly things like this:

```
OOXXOO    and        EE
ZZ  ZZ            YY  YY
```

That wasn't getting him anywhere, was it? And it seemed to irritate Peeper, who was sitting on the table watching as usual. In fact, it irritated her so much that she kept on pawing at the paper, and that drew Bobby's attention to her and gave him his idea at last. So although it was time to go to bed, he typed the following words at the top of a fresh sheet of paper:

MY CAT

Then he left the sheet in the typewriter ready to compose his essay when he felt fresh the next morning.

In the middle of the night another very funny thing happened. While he was asleep in bed he thought he heard the tap-tapping of his typewriter. He was dozing at the time, and the tapping was so regular and soothing that it sent him off to sleep again, and by the time he woke up in the morning he had forgotten all about it. But not for long. When he dressed and went to look on his table, what do you think he saw? His typewriter with a full sheet of typing on it, headed by the two words he himself had typed the night before. This is what it said:

MY CAT

I am a cat and I belong to Bobby
Brewster. At least, he thinks I belong
to him, but in fact I belong to no one
but myself. Mind you, I like Bobby
Brewster, he is a very nice boy and I
often purr when I am sitting on his
lap. But only when I feel like purring
not just because he wants me to purr.

13

He gave me a funny name when I was young. He called me 'Peeper'. That was because when I tried to say 'miaow' it sounded like 'peep'. And what's wrong with that? Even now I am older I still say 'peep' because I think it sounds nicer than 'miaow'.

One of the other things Bobby noticed when we first met was that I looked like a squirrel. That was because I had – and still have – a long bushy tail, grey fur all over me and a tiny head with very small ears. When he first saw me he thought that I looked so much like a squirrel that he said, 'You aren't a proper kitten at all, you're a squitten.' Now I am older I suppose he must think I'm a squat.

Sometimes when I was a squitten I was rather silly. I chased flies and ran up curtains and tangled balls of wool and got inside paper bags. Between you and me I still like getting inside paper bags because they make a funny rustling noise when I wriggle my paws, and when I get the chance I still tangle balls of wool because it annoys Bobby's mother, and she looks so funny when she is annoyed.

Of course, human beings, especially grown-ups, often look funny to cats, although they don't realize it. They take everything so seriously don't

they, and make such an awful fuss.
Cats don't. They simply draw themselves up in dignified silence and
stalk off, which is far more effect-
ive. Occasionally they may hiss, but
only at other cats who are presuming.

And what jobs human beings find
themselves to do! Like washing up,
with all that foamy hot water. Cats
don't. They just lick their plate
clean and walk away and leave it.
That's if they approve of what they
were given to eat in the first place,
which is by no means always the case.
And if they don't approve, they make
their feelings quite clear by the
expression of complete and utter
disdain on their faces when they leave
the food untouched.

Then when grown-ups are going to a
party, there is such a palaver before-
hand – baths, clean clothes, brushing
of hair, scent behind the ears, and
all that nonsense, and even after that
they often have a long car journey.
Cats don't. They just find a warm
spot, lick themselves all over carefully with their convenient prickly
tongues and glide away to meet other
cats. And they all look just as spruce
and smart as people and enjoy themselves just as much with far less
effort.

No, all things considered, cats are
far more sensible than humans. They

do just what they like, when they like, where they like and with whom they like. With half-closed eyes, in relaxed attitudes, they take everything in and then decide for themselves and act accordingly. And if you know any humans who have the sense to behave like that, I should be very surprised.

Bobby read it and re-read it in amazement. Can I have typed it in my sleep? he thought.

He had to admit that it was very unlikely because it seemed a far better essay than he had ever composed before. But who else knew so much about Peeper? And who else knew so much about his typewriter? There was only one possible answer. Peeper herself had typed an essay about herself.

Bobby didn't tell anyone. As a matter of fact he felt rather relieved because he still didn't feel in a composing mood himself.

The following day, he handed in that essay, and it was two days before Mr Limcano made his announcement.

'Well, children,' he said, 'I am glad you all took so much trouble with your weekend essays. I read them with great interest, but for once I had no difficulty in deciding who should have the prize or what the prize would be. Bobby Brewster handed in an essay about his cat which is so realistic that it might have been written by the cat herself, so I think she is the one who deserves the prize.'

And then, amidst much laughter, he handed Bobby Brewster a tin of cat food.

Counting sheep

Bobby Brewster was very anxious to go to sleep quickly one night last year. It was the day before Prizegiving Day, and for once he had actually won a prize – for coming top in Nature Study, of all things. He was rather excited at the prospect, and went to bed early so that the next day would come all the sooner. But it didn't, because he couldn't get off to sleep. First, he had a tickle in his throat, and then his nose started itching. After that he had a tummy rumble, probably because in his excitement he had eaten his supper of bread and cheese too quickly. He tossed and turned and told himself not to be so restless, but he kept thinking about walking up on to that platform the next day and being given his prize in front of all those people. Although he felt tired, his mind just wouldn't stop working.

Then he had an idea. Someone had told him

that the best way of falling asleep was to count imaginary sheep going through an imaginary gate.

Very well, he said to himself, I will start counting sheep. So he did. He screwed his eyes tight, concentrated on sheep, and started to count.

One–two–three–four–five.

Then a very funny thing happened. He heard a loud 'B-a-a'. At least, not just one 'B-a-a', but lots of them, all in different voices.

'B-a-a. B-a-a. B-a-a. B-a-a.'

He opened his eyes in surprise – and he was even more surprised when he looked towards his bedroom door. It wasn't a bedroom door any more. It was really a gate, swinging to and fro on its hinges. And there were sheep going through it, all pushing and shoving as only sheep can push and shove.

How on earth can they have got here? Bobby asked himself. They must have found the front door open and scampered up the stairs.

Then he thought again. How did they get to the front door in the first place? The nearest farm with sheep on it is several miles away on the other side of the town. And what about my mother and father? Surely they can hear all this noise? And, if so, why aren't they worried about the sheep kicking the front door and spreading mud all up the staircase carpet?

Bobby couldn't possibly count the sheep. There were far too many of them, all trying to push through the gate at once. They jostled against the side of his bed, kicked over the bedroom chair, pushed into the cupboard, and clambered on to the chest of drawers. One of them started drinking the lemonade from the glass he always keeps on his bedside table, and another chewed the tail of his shirt which was hanging over the end of his bed.

And the noise they were making!

'B-a-a. B-a-a. B-a-a.' It really was quite terrifying. Bobby wondered what on earth he could do to stop it.

He needn't have worried. His problem was solved for him. The next moment he suddenly realized that he wasn't in bed any more. He was sitting in the second row in the school hall, looking expectantly up at the platform. How on

earth he came to be there he hadn't the slightest idea, but there he undoubtedly was. And there weren't any children in the hall, or parents either. It was full of sheep! On one side of the gangway, where the children usually sit on Prizegiving Days – and where Bobby himself was sitting – were lots of lambs, bleating excitedly in high-pitched voices. And on the parents' side were rows of serious-looking father and mother sheep making quiet conversational bleats. Some of the mother sheep were wearing very smart hats, the sort that mothers are apt to wear at prize-givings.

Then everything was suddenly quiet as an important-looking ram with great swirling horns above his ears climbed on to the platform. He had a heavy gold chain round his neck, and was wearing horn-rimmed spectacles.

'B-a-a,' said the important ram in a deep voice, and the audience hushed respectfully.

'B-a-a, B-a-a, B-a-a,' continued the mayor ram in a speechified voice, which wasn't really surprising because it soon became clear that he really was making a speech. And a very good speech it must have been, judging by the reactions of the audience. They kept on making restrained sheep laughs – 'B-a—a—a. B-a—a—a.' Even Bobby found the speech quite amusing, although he couldn't understand a word of it. Even so, it was certainly far more interesting than the speech the vicar had made at the prize-giving the year before.

Then the ram stopped his speech, looked down from the platform, and announced with a loud bleat, 'B-o-b-b-y B-r-e-w-s-t-e-r.'

Bobby nearly jumped out of his skin, and the lambs sitting near all turned towards him.

'B-o-b-b-y B-r-e-w-s-t-e-r,' re-bleated the

mayor, shaking his horns impatiently and looking down the hall over his spectacles.

Bobby marched towards the platform, and the audience bleated its congratulations.

What on earth is he going to give me for a prize? thought Bobby. He might well have asked – and I am sure you will never guess either. His prize was a plate of bread and cheese!

This is ridiculous, thought Bobby, standing up

on the platform with a plate of bread and cheese in one hand and a knife in the other. And am I supposed to eat it in front of all these people?

No – apparently he wasn't. Once again, his problem was solved for him because he found that he was back in bed, and his bedroom was even more full of sheep than it had been when he was whisked away to the school hall. They were climbing all round the room and bleating piteously.

Oh dear, oh dear! thought Bobby. What *can* I do? I must have sheep on the brain. Whoever told me that counting sheep would help me to get to sleep was talking absolute nonsense. I can't get away from the wretched sheep anywhere, and counting them is quite out of the question!

Now whether those sheep could read his thoughts or not I don't know, but at that very moment another one of his problems was solved. The sheep started to count themselves. They did, really. One by one they trailed out of the bedroom gate and down the stairs, and as they pushed the gate open they announced their own number in bleating voices:

'O-n-e. T-w-o. T-h-r-e-e. F-o-o-u-r. F-i-i-v-e. S-i-i-x. S-e-e-e-ven. E-i-i-i-ght.'

By the time the n-i-i-inth sheep went through the gate Bobby Brewster was fast asleep in his bed. And how many more sheep after that announced their number as they went through the gate he will never know, because when he woke up the next morning his bedroom had a proper door once more and there was not a single sheep in sight.

Two more funny things happened on Prize-giving Day. As Bobby tripped up to the platform he nearly had a fit of the giggles. The mayor, who was presenting the prizes, had a heavy gold chain round his neck and was wearing horn-rimmed spectacles. He looked almost exactly like the ram of the night before, except of course that there were no horns growing above his ears. Bobby hardly knew where to look as he was handed a lovely book for his prize. It was The Children's Encyclopaedia of British Animals. When he returned to his seat he opened it to look at the pictures. Then he really did have a fit of the giggles. The first picture he saw was of a magnificent ram. It had fine horns above its ears, and it looked almost exactly like the mayor, except, of course, that there was no heavy gold chain round its neck and it wasn't wearing horn-rimmed spectacles.

Clothes on the line

'I *know* you're going to a picnic party this afternoon, Bobby,' said his mother one fine morning, 'and I realize that you're excited about it, but *please* stop talking and leave me alone to get on with the washing. It's a lovely day, and I want to hang it up on the line as quickly as possible while there's a good breeze blowing.'

Bobby went out into the garden slightly abashed, but only slightly. After all, he had merely mentioned the picnic party to pass the time. He had been to a party before and been on a picnic, but a picnic party – that was something new and extra exciting. Oh dear, would the afternoon never come!

Then he had an idea. He could offer to be helpful. His mother couldn't possibly object to that, and it might make the morning pass all the more quickly. So he ran back into the kitchen.

'Mother,' he started.

'What is it now?' asked his mother in a resigned voice.

'Let me hang up the washing for you,' suggested Bobby. 'Then you can get on with your second load in the washing machine.'

His mother looked doubtful. 'Show me your hands first,' she said, and Bobby held them up. 'Not at all bad for once,' said his mother. 'Well, thank you, Bobby, it's very kind of you. Remember to use plenty of pegs and don't let the clothes drag on the grass. Here's the first basket load.'

Bobby lugged the heavy basket on to the back lawn, and started to hang up the washing on the line which hung between two trees. As soon as he had finished, he stood back to admire his handiwork and saw all the clothes dancing happily in the breeze. At least, he thought they were happy until a very funny thing happened.

A voice shouted, 'Stop it!'

'I beg your pardon?' asked Bobby.

And the voice snapped back, 'I'm not talking to you.'

Well, that's a relief anyway, thought Bobby. If he *had* been talking to me, I wouldn't have known what to stop. But I wonder who it is.

He soon found out. The voice shouted again much more loudly. 'Stop it, I said.' And Bobby realized to his surprise that it came from his father's shirt on the line.

He was even more surprised when he saw the reason for the shouting. There was a gust of wind and one of his own grey woollen socks with a red stripe round the top jerked across and gave the tail of his father's shirt a great big kick.

'That hurt!' shouted the shirt, but it immediately had its revenge. With the next gust of wind it swung back with its two free arms and caught hold of the socks and pulled violently.

'You're choking us,' howled the socks.

'I must put a stop to this at once,' decided Bobby, and he unpegged the offending sock, which had, after all started the quarrel, and carried it over to the end of the line where it was hung in disgrace all by itself.

'That'll teach you to kick people,' said Bobby,

29

and, as he said it, the sock swung viciously and kicked him on the arm.

'Now really,' protested Bobby. 'Why are you in such a vicious temper this morning?'

'It's all your fault,' snapped the sock.

'I beg your pardon?' asked Bobby Brewster.

'I said, it's all your fault,' repeated the sock.

'My fault!' cried Bobby. 'All I've done is to help my mother by hanging out the washing.'

'Not until you'd talked the hind legs off a donkey,' said the sock crossly. 'No wonder your mother turned you out of the kitchen. Yap, yap, yap, all about some marvellous picnic party you're going to.'

'Well, you'd talk if you were going to a picnic party,' said Bobby.

'That's the whole point,' answered the sock, 'we're not. You're already wearing the clothes that are going to the picnic party with you and we're going to be left here stuck on the line. It's not fair.'

'I don't know about that,' commented Bobby. 'It must be jolly good fun dancing on the line in a cool breeze. Besides I couldn't possibly wear three pairs of socks, three shirts, four pairs of pants and four vests to a party, could I? I should look silly and get far too hot.'

'The fact remains that it isn't fair,' argued the sock. 'Why did you choose those particular clothes to wear for your picnic party, anyway?'

'I didn't choose them,' protested Bobby. 'They happened to be on top when I opened my chest of drawers.'

31

'It's still not fair,' repeated the sock obstinately.

Then Bobby Brewster had an idea. 'I can quite understand your disappointment,' he said, 'but, of course, I can't possibly change my clothes before the party. For one thing you wouldn't be dry enough to wear, and for another it wouldn't be fair to the clothes I *am* wearing at the moment, because they have already been promised a treat. But I'll tell you what I'll do. First of all, I'll ask Mrs Henderson next door if she will allow me to hang you up on her clothes line today. That'll make a nice change for you, won't it?'

'Well, I suppose it will,' agreed the sock doubtfully, 'but we're still going to be stuck up with pegs, aren't we?'

'Certainly,' agreed Bobby. 'But a change of scene is always refreshing. Besides, I haven't finished yet. While you're hanging on Mrs Henderson's line, I want you to find out for me what parties all the clothes like best. Then I'll try and arrange to wear them in future on their own special days.'

'Now that really *is* a good idea,' said the sock.

'Leave it to me. I'll discuss it with my friends while you're out this afternoon.'

Well, first of all, of course, Bobby had to explain to his mother and Mrs Henderson about using Mrs Henderson's clothes line without giving away his magic. He got round it by saying that there was such a lot of washing to hang up that day that to spread it really properly more lines were necessary. They both thought it rather a peculiar idea, but just to keep him quiet they agreed. And as a matter of fact it worked out very well. The clothes hung so freely that they had an extra airing, and, since then, Mrs Brewster and Mrs Henderson always arrange to do their washing on different days so that they can use both lines.

When the washing was collected the next day, and after it had been ironed and stacked in the airing cupboard, Bobby took his socks with the red-striped tops into his bedroom. Then, when he was quite sure no one could hear him, he asked anxiously, 'Well, have you found out what I want?'

There was no need to be anxious because one

sock answered at once, quite distinctly. 'Yes,' it said. 'Get a piece of paper and a pencil. It's quite a long list.'

So Bobby wrote down all the instructions as they were given to him.

Tartan shirts like tea parties.
White shirts wedding parties.
Blue shirts like birthday parties.
Check shirts like Christmas parties.

34

Purple shirts like picnic parties.

Pink shirts like pantomime parties.

Vests like any sort of party, as long as they don't get too hot.

Pants don't mind what parties they go to because they can't see anyway. They prefer to hang on the line.

'Right,' said Bobby, when he had written the list. 'I'll keep this carefully and see what I can do to arrange matters.'

Ever since then he has followed those instructions very carefully. Sometimes it has been rather difficult when he has been trying to persuade his mother that he must wear one particular shirt to one particular party without giving away the magic reason. And on one occasion during last Christmas holidays, it was really very embarrassing. He wore his cheerful new pink shirt to its first pantomime, and it laughed so loudly at all the funny bits that people sitting round him stared in amazement. So as not to give anything away, Bobby had to pretend he was roaring with laughter instead of his pink shirt,

35

and at first it made him feel rather silly. He soon cheered up, though, because his laughter proved so infectious that it set everyone else laughing as well, and the result was that all the people in the theatre that afternoon thoroughly enjoyed the pantomime.

What is a weed?

Mr Brewster – that's Bobby's father – isn't very good at gardening, I'm afraid, but there is *one* thing he doesn't mind doing, and that is mowing the lawn. At least, he *calls* it the lawn, but real gardeners might describe it more accurately as a field cut short, because it is full of daisies, buttercups, dandelions, clover, with the occasional thistle thrown in for luck.

He uses a motor mower – rather a temperamental one – which only works when it feels like it, and mending motor mowers is another thing that Mr Brewster isn't very good at. So the state of the lawn depends on the state of the motor mower, and the state of the motor mower depends on getting hold of a man to mend it when it goes wrong.

And, curiously enough, the state of Mr Brewster *after* mowing the lawn used to depend on the state of one particular apple tree. Now that may sound ridiculous, so let me explain.

Six apple trees grow on the bank at the bottom of the lawn. Some years they grow lots of apples, and some years none at all. When the crop is good, Bobby's mother cooks apple pie and stewed apples until the Brewsters have apple coming out of their ears. And Bobby's father stores apples on racks in the shed, many of which develop wrinkles, go rotten, and have to be thrown away.

But to return to the particular apple tree. Some time ago Mr Brewster finally decided that it didn't like him. You see, when he mowed the lawn underneath this tree, it seemed to object. As he walked beneath it with the mower the branches clutched at his sleeves and tore his shirt. Every time, as he steered beneath that tree, he stooped lower and lower to avoid the branches, and every time one of the branches tore at him viciously. Once he even broke off the end of a branch in a temper after it had torn his shirt, but it did no good. The next time he mowed the lawn another branch of the tree did the tearing. It was absolutely infuriating, and he was convinced that the tree did it on purpose. Of course, he only said that in fun, but, as a matter of fact, had he known as much about magic as his son Bobby, he would have realized that what he said was perfectly true.

Bobby Brewster found out about it one day two summers ago. I'm not going to tell you what his father was saying that day about that apple tree as he came in from mowing the lawn, but it was certainly not complimentary. One of the branches had torn at his hair and made a vivid red scratch across the top of his head, so Mrs Brewster had to daub it with T.C.P., and

that made Mr Brewster repeat some of the expressions he had been using before.

Bobby ran down the garden and stood looking at the apple tree, wondering to himself whether it could really have scratched his father's head on purpose. At least, he *thought* he was wondering to himself, but he couldn't have been, because a gruff voice said, 'It serves him right.'

'I beg your pardon?' asked Bobby Brewster.

'I said it serves him right,' repeated the voice.

'What serves who right?' asked Bobby.

'Scratching serves your father right,' said the voice.

'Who are you?' asked Bobby, in amazement.

'I'm the apple tree you're staring at,' said the voice. 'And you can tell your father from me that I'm glad I scratched his head, and when he next mows the lawn I shall try and scratch it again.'

'You're very unkind,' protested Bobby. 'What has my father done to you?'

'Nothing actually to me,' said the apple tree. 'It's what he does to my friends that I object to.'

'What friends?' asked Bobby.

'My friends the buttercups and daisies and dandelions and clover and thistles,' explained the tree. 'As soon as they grow up, he comes along with that silly motor mower of his and cuts their heads off.'

'He *has* to mow the lawn to keep it tidy,' cried Bobby. 'And, anyway, buttercups and daisies and dandelions and clover and thistles are weeds.'

'Who said so?' asked the tree.

'I did,' said Bobby.

'And what do you mean by weeds?' demanded the tree.

'Well ... things like daisies and buttercups and dandelions,' explained Bobby. At least, he *thought* he was explaining. But, when you come to think of it, was he?

'That's ridiculous,' said the tree. 'Daisies and buttercups and dandelions are lovely flowers. Have you ever looked at them closely?'

'Not closely,' admitted Bobby. 'But when I was younger I made daisy chains and hung them round my neck. And people held buttercups under my chin to see if I was fond of butter.'

41

'And were you?' asked the tree.

'Very,' said Bobby. 'And I still am.'

'Then I think it's most thoughtless of you to be so rude about daisies and buttercups and call them weeds,' said the apple tree. '*I* think they are beautiful little flowers. And they're so cheerful and friendly, like the cocky sparrows and perky robins. Far more friendly than that snooty rose over there in the border. Just because she looks and smells nice she thinks she's everybody.'

'Well – she *is* lovely,' said Bobby.

'So she jolly well ought to be with all the trouble Pethers, your gardener, takes,' said the tree. 'Watering her, and putting manure all round her, and fussing over her. And she doesn't even thank Pethers for it. She thinks she's God's gift to nature.'

'So she is, in a way,' said Bobby.

'Yes, and so are the daisies and buttercups and dandelions and clover and thistles. And so am I. And so are you, for that matter.'

'That's true, I suppose,' agreed Bobby – and he hoped his mother and father were always of the same opinion.

'Then go away and think,' said the apple tree. 'And see what you can do about it.'

Before he went back to the house Bobby stopped to look at some daisies that were pushing up their cheeky heads on the top corner of the lawn. He picked one and counted the clear white petals. There were forty-seven of them. Then he tried to count the little yellow bobbles clustered in a neat circle in the middle, but he had to give that up because there were so many that counting made him dizzy. Even the underneath of the flower was fascinating, with a slender stem form-

ing a sort of wine-glass of thirteen tiny leaves carrying the pink tinted petals. The whole effect was, in its way, quite perfect. Then Bobby picked a dandelion. Now dandelions are considered by serious gardeners to be real pests, but aren't they beautiful flowers? The dandelion that Bobby studied had all the glory of the sun in it, widening from a deep gold in the centre to a dazzling yellow on the tips of the petals and backed delicately with tender leaves. Then Bobby decided. To call such beautiful things weeds simply wasn't fair.

He ran back to the house and found his father still mopping the tree scratch on top of his head.

'Father,' he asked. 'What is a weed?'

His father was taken aback with the sudden question, but he answered rather lamely, 'Well, I suppose buttercups and daisies are weeds.'

'Why?' asked Bobby promptly.

'What do you mean, "why?"?' asked his father.

'Why should a daisy be a weed any more than a rose?' demanded Bobby. 'It's a lovely flower.'

Mr Brewster didn't want to get into an argument where he wasn't sure of himself, so he suggested that they should look up the word 'weed' in an encyclopaedia. It said 'Wild plants growing in cultivated ground.'

Bobby looked thoughtful, and then said, 'That doesn't really answer anything. What about the primroses and daffodils on our lawn? When they flower in the spring do you call them weeds?'

'Of course not,' said his father. 'They're not wild flowers. I suppose the simplest description of weeds is, "Plants growing where they're not wanted".'

'And who doesn't want them?' asked Bobby.

'I don't for one,' said his father. 'I don't want daisies on my lawn for instance.'

'But I *do* like daisies on the lawn,' said Bobby, 'so they may be weeds to you, but to me they are wild flowers.'

Mr Brewster felt that he was getting rather out of his depth, and he said, a little doubtfully, 'Yes, I suppose that's true.'

'Very well,' continued Bobby, who was now feeling excited about a new idea. 'May I have the top right-hand corner of the lawn for myself?

It's behind the apple tree and doesn't show from here, and it's already full of daisies. I want to grow more daisies and buttercups and dandelions and other plants that you call weeds and I don't. I've been looking at some of them more closely this morning, and I don't think it's fair to call them weeds, so I want a wild flower garden of my own.'

Well, although he wasn't sure whether it was wise or not, Bobby's father could hardly refuse, could he? After all, Bobby had worked out the idea all for himself, and, when you come to think of it, it wasn't a bad idea, was it? As long as Bobby didn't allow his wild plants to spread all over the garden.

'Very well,' said his father, after a little thought. 'You may have your top corner of the lawn. But look after it properly, and don't let your weeds . . .'

'Wild flowers, please,' corrected Bobby.

'Sorry – wild flowers,' continued his father. 'Don't let them get out of control.'

So that is what Bobby did. It wasn't as easy as he thought it would be. Some weeds really are

weeds wherever they grow. Bindweed, for instance. It began to spread selfishly all over Bobby's corner and stifle the other flowers, and Bobby had to destroy it as best he could, although it always tried to creep back again. And it was a funny thing. Some of the other wild flowers in the district seemed to get to hear of it, so they came where they knew they were wanted, and Bobby's garden became quite famous in time, with its wealth of colour. And the daisies, buttercups, and dandelions on the middle of the Brewsters' lawn began to realize they weren't wanted

47

there, so they shifted to Bobby's corner where they could hold up their heads proudly as wild flowers.

Another funny thing happened, too. Bobby often wondered if the talk he'd had with the apple tree was really his imagination, and that I cannot say for sure. But the fact remains that now Bobby's wild flowers are allowed to flourish, branches of that apple tree never clutch viciously at Mr Brewster as he mows the lawn. Indeed, they seem to sway apart and allow him to guide his mower underneath without even having to stoop at all. And never again has his shirt been torn or his head been scratched. What is more, the motor mower seems to work far more smoothly now that it has no daisies, buttercups and dandelions in the middle of the lawn to cut the heads from.

So now everyone is satisfied. Mr Brewster is satisfied with his motor mower. The apple tree is satisfied with Mr Brewster. Bobby Brewster is satisfied with his garden of wild flowers. And, now that you have finished reading it, I hope you are satisfied with my story.

With knobs on

When you are walking along a road beside some iron railings I can guess something that you often do. You trail a stick along the railings, and make a *brrrr*-ing noise, don't you?

And you are not the only one. Who else do you think does that? Why, Bobby Brewster of course. What is more, he has the chance of doing it every day, because on his way to school he has to pass a stretch of railings on the edge of a park. He *brrrrs* very methodically, too. He even keeps a special stick for this purpose. On his way to school he finds his stick stuck in the earth at the beginning of the railings, and when he has finished his *brrrr*-ing he sticks it in the earth at the other end ready to pull out on his return journey. Then he *brrrs* again on his way home and leaves the stick ready for collection the following morning.

Bobby has become quite an expert at ringing – or rather *brrrr*-ing the changes. The noise depends on how much time he has. When he is late and has to run, the *brrrr* along the railings is long and high-pitched. And if it is raining, the drops of water spray outwards as the stick dislodges them. Once, on a day that was bright and raining at the same time, Bobby even managed to make his own rainbow of spray.

On the way home he can dawdle and use his stick on and off the railings to make a pattern of dot and dash brrrrs. He can trail the stick high, low, or in the middle, and occasionally only tap every other railing. Sometimes it almost sounds as if the railings are talking to him.

Did I say, 'talking'? Well, I was nearer the truth than I realized because, one morning, a very funny thing happened.

It was the day before Bobby's birthday and he was wondering what present his mother and father were going to give him. Was it going to be something useful like a pullover or a pair of socks? Or was it going to be something unexpected and exciting to play with? You can guess which of those types he hoped for, can't you? Sometime or other they would *have* to buy him a pullover or stockings, wouldn't they, birthday or no birthday.

That morning he had left for school with plenty of time to spare. When he reached the park he thought he would make a change from simple *brrrr*-ing, and count the railings as he banged them one at a time.

He had never counted them before and decided in his mind that there couldn't possibly be more than a hundred of them. In fact he was so certain that he said to himself, 'If there *are* more than a hundred, I shan't be given an exciting birthday present to play with, but only something useful.'

As he was reaching the end of the railings it became clear that he had misjudged. He had already called number 'eighty-nine', and there were certainly far more than twelve to come. Oh dear – he *did* so badly want an exciting birthday present, and he wouldn't get one if he counted over one hundred railings.

So he started counting backwards. 'Eighty-eight. Eighty-seven. Eighty-six.' Then a very

funny thing happened. A voice said, 'That's cheating.'

'I beg your pardon?' asked Bobby Brewster.

'I said, "that's cheating",' repeated the voice.

'Who are you?' asked Bobby, in surprise.

'I'm number ninety-one, and you just called me eighty-seven,' said the voice. 'That's cheating, and I object.'

'Why?' asked Bobby. 'One railing's just like another railing.'

'You're not very observant, are you, young

man?' said the voice. 'If you looked properly you would see that I'm not just a railing at all. I'm far more important. I'm a metal post with a strong bracket at my base and a smart knob on my top. Without me and the other metal posts the whole row of railings would collapse. Only we posts are securely fixed in the ground, and only we posts have brackets at the base and knobs on top.'

'So you have,' agreed Bobby. 'I had never noticed that before. And very smart knobs they are too. They are shaped like acorns.'

'Even more than that,' continued the voice. 'I'm the most important post of all the posts with knobs on, because I'm magic.'

'You jolly well must be, if you can talk,' said Bobby. 'But I still don't see what difference it makes calling you number eighty-seven instead of ninety-one.'

'It's not *true*, that's the difference,' protested the post. 'And there's another thing. I object to all this *brrr*-ing of yours twice a day. It hurts.'

'Oh, come now,' said Bobby in a soothing voice. 'Surely a fine strong metal post like you can't be hurt by a gentle little *brrrr*.'

'Your stick scratches the paint,' complained the post. 'And even when it doesn't hurt, it tickles. Anyway, why are you counting us at all this morning? I don't see that it matters how many of us there are.'

'It matters to me,' said Bobby.

'Why?' demanded the post.

'Because it's my birthday tomorrow,' explained Bobby, 'and I have decided that if there are more than a hundred railings, my father and mother will give me a useful present and not an exciting one. And I'm afraid that there *are* more than a hundred.'

'More than a hundred what?' asked the metal post.

'More than a hundred railings,' said Bobby. 'You're already really number ninety-one, and there are at least twenty more. And that comes to a total of one hundred and eleven. So that's why I started counting backwards.'

'Well it was very silly of you,' said the post indignantly. 'For one thing it's cheating, and cheating never works in the end. And for another there are *not* over one hundred railings.'

'Oh, come now,' said Bobby. 'Surely if you're magic you can count properly. Ninety-one plus twenty *is* one hundred and eleven you know.'

'Yes, but you see,' said the post knowingly, 'I'm *not* the ninety-first railing. In fact, as I said before, I'm not a railing at all. I'm far more important than a mere railing. I'm a metal post with a smart acorn knob on top. And if you will take the trouble to look you will find that every row

of nine railings is held at each end by a metal post with a knob on top.'

Bobby counted quickly on to the next post with a knob on top.

'You know, you're quite right,' he agreed. 'There *are* nine railings in each row.'

'Of course I'm right,' snapped the metal post. 'What's the good of being magic if you can't be right?'

'But even that doesn't help much,' continued Bobby. 'There are two whole sets of railings after you, so surely they *must* count up to over one hundred.'

'You may be surprised to know that you're wrong,' explained the post. 'But only just. Although you *could* count up to one hundred and eleven altogether, that includes twelve metal posts with knobs on. So how many ordinary railings does that leave?'

Bobby thought hard. 'Why, *ninety-nine*,' he cried excitedly. 'Just one less than a hundred. So I *shall* get an exciting birthday present after all.'

'Well, at least there's a chance of it,' said the post.

'Thank you *very* much for explaining it,' said Bobby. 'You really *are* magic. If ever a metal post *deserved* to have a smart acorn knob on top, it's you.'

'That's all right,' said the magic post modestly. 'I didn't make *myself* magic you know. It just happened that way. So I'm lucky.'

Well, of course Bobby could hardly wait for his birthday. At school that day he twice had to be spoken to rather sharply by Mr Limcano because his mind was on birthday presents instead of lessons. And that night, as he usually does when he wants the next day to come all the sooner, he went to bed early.

Birthday morning dawned bright and Bobby woke early. Where do you think he looked when he first opened his eyes and realized what day it was? On his bedside table of course. And what do you think he saw there? A large parcel wrapped in fancy paper, with a label on the string saying,

Many happy returns, Bobby,
with love from Mother and Father.

I'm afraid he didn't unknot the string and fold up the paper neatly. He used his penknife to cut the knot and tore open the wrapping excitedly. It was a box of the most marvellous wooden skittles. Ten-pin skittles – a game that Bobby loves playing and sometimes plays quite well. But, even more surprising, can you guess what was on top of each skittle?

A smart acorn knob!

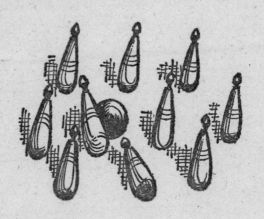

The piece of chalk

It all started on a very ordinary day which was hardly surprising because Bobby Brewster is just an ordinary boy. To be exact, it was on Tuesday, February 19th, and what could be more ordinary than that? Tuesday is the most ordinary day in the week – exciting things just don't seem to happen on Tuesdays. The 19th day isn't at the beginning or end of the month, or even right in the middle. It's just the 19th day. As for February – well, what less exciting month of the year can there be? Except, of course, for people with February birthdays, and it was on an extra special birthday that this story started.

The children arrived for school that morning rather cold and miserable because there was a driving wind and sleet in the air. They were allowed in the classrooms early before assembly to get out of the wet. As you know, Bobby

Brewster is in Mr Limcano's class, and as soon as he entered the classroom he cheered up, because of an exciting announcement in chalk on the blackboard:

TUESDAY, FEBRUARY 19th
MANY HAPPY RETURNS OF THE DAY
TO MR LIMCANO
FROM CLASS 2A

The other children cheered up as well, and they all waited anxiously for the arrival of Mr Limcano himself. Then, as he opened the classroom door, without any prompting they stood up and sang with one accord,

'*Happy birthday to you!*
Happy birthday to you!
Happy birthday, Mr Limcano,
Happy birthday to you!'

Mr Limcano beamed all over his face and blushed.

'Thank you, children,' he said. 'What a nice way to start such a miserable day. But how did you know it was my birthday?'

'From the announcement on the blackboard,' said Bobby.

Mr Limcano looked at the blackboard in surprise.

'Who wrote that?' he asked, but nobody answered.

'Come now, somebody must have written it,' persisted Mr Limcano.

'*I* didn't, sir,' said Bobby, and his remark was followed by lots of 'Nor did I's'.

'What an extraordinary thing,' said Mr Limcano. 'Never mind, it's perfectly true, and your welcome has already made it a very happy birthday. But I don't want the whole school to know, so let's keep it a secret just for 2A, shall we? I will rub this out and we must all go along to assembly.'

After that, they forgot all about the mysterious writing on the blackboard. Then, on the following Monday, which was also a miserable day, another funny thing happened. When the children were let in early they read on the board an even more exciting notice.

MONDAY FEBRUARY 25th
AFTER ASSEMBLY
CLASS 2A GIVE THREE CHEERS
FOR MISS TRENHAM

Mr Limcano arrived in a rush at the last minute because his car had taken a long time to start, and he led the children straight along to the hall without even setting out his desk. Assembly went as usual with prayers and a very appropriate hymn for that particular day – 'In the bleak midwinter'. Then, as soon as Miss Trenham on the platform said, 'Thank you children, that is the end of our assembly,' Bobby Brewster, who was sitting with his class in the middle of the hall, stood up and shouted, '2A, three cheers for Miss Trenham,' and there followed three resounding cheers from the whole of 2A.

The rest of the children in the school and all the teachers standing along the side of the hall were extremely surprised, and as for Miss Trenham on the platform, she looked absolutely amazed.

'It's very kind of you, Bobby,' she said when she recovered, 'but what were those cheers for?'

'For you, Miss Trenham,' said Bobby.

'I realized that because I heard you say so, but why today of all days?'

'Because we were asked to give three cheers for Miss Trenham,' said Bobby.

'But who asked you?' insisted Miss Trenham.

'A notice on our classroom blackboard,' explained Bobby, and Miss Trenham looked at Mr Limcano.

'I didn't write the notice,' he said, 'nor have I seen one. I think we had better investigate.' So all the children filed back to their classrooms, and Mr Limcano and Miss Trenham went with 2A.

'Now children,' asked Miss Trenham, when she read the notice on the blackboard, 'whose writing is this?' The only reply she received was a chorus of, 'Not mine, Miss!'

Miss Trenham looked rather severe.

'I suppose no one wants to own up to doing such a silly thing,' she said. 'Well, I will overlook it this time, but do not let it happen again. Cheers are all very flattering in their place, but not at

assembly on a wet Monday morning for no reason at all.' And she walked stiffly out of the room.

Everyone was subdued after that, and may well have remained so because the children were ashamed of Miss Trenham's rebuke, although they still didn't know who was responsible for the notice on the blackboard.

Then the situation was completely transformed.

'You all seem a bit dull this morning,' said Mr Limcano, 'so to wake you up I'm going to ask you some snap questions on all sorts of subjects. But think before you speak. I want correct answers, and we will see who can answer them the quickest. The first question is about the new currency. If you bought four pounds of apples at ten pence a pound and two melons at thirteen pence each, how much change would you get from a pound note?'

As the children were working it out in their heads, a very funny thing happened. Behind Mr Limcano's back, a piece of chalk jumped up from the ledge beneath the blackboard, and without any of the usual chalk squeak it wrote the answer neatly for all of the class:

34 p

'Thirty-four pence,' cried all the children.

Mr Limcano was quite taken aback. 'You are not as dull as I thought you were,' he said. 'Now let's try history. Which king signed Magna Carta?'

Most of the children hadn't the slightest idea, but it didn't matter in the least. Up jumped the piece of chalk and wrote:

KING JOHN

'King John, sir,' cried the children all together, and Mr Limcano was very gratified.

'I'm a better teacher than I thought I was,' he said. 'Now I'll ask you one which I'm sure you don't all know. What is the capital of Sweden?'

No one knew the answer to that. They looked eagerly at the blackboard as the piece of chalk was writing and in the middle cried:

STOCK

Mr Limcano noticed all their eyes concentrating in one direction and swung round just in time to see the chalk finishing the word with:

HOLM

'Goodness gracious me!' he cried, and tried to grab the piece of chalk. But it escaped his clutches, ran down the wall, and along the floor. Mr Limcano dashed after it as the children cheered. He stumbled and trod on the end of it, and the remaining piece of chalk rushed along the floor and disappeared.

'Where on earth has it gone?' asked Mr Limcano.

Then Bobby Brewster had an idea.

'Follow the trail of the chalk and you will find it, sir,' he suggested. So Mr Limcano got on all fours and crawled round the classroom following the line made by the escaping chalk, and traced it to the waste paper basket.

'Got it!' he yelled, and held up the piece of chalk triumphantly. But it was only a tiddly little piece because he had trodden on one end and turned it into chalk dust.

'Oh, sir!' cried the children accusingly. 'It was magic, and you trod on it!'

'I'm sorry about that,' replied Mr Limcano, 'but how on earth was I to know? Whoever heard of a magic piece of chalk writing its own messages and answers before?'

There was no answer to that, was there? After

all whoever *did* hear of such an extraordinary thing?

Mr Limcano put the piece of chalk back on the ledge beneath the blackboard.

'This is an extra-precious article,' he said. 'The wisest thing to do first of all is to test it and make sure that it really is as magic as we think it is. Then we must decide where to keep it and how best to use it.'

He thought hard and added, 'Now then, what shall I ask? Something that no one of us could possibly answer at once out of our own head.'

Bobby Brewster promptly held his hand up. Trust Bobby Brewster!

'Please, sir,' he asked. 'What is 1632 multiplied by 47?'

'I'm sure I don't know,' said Mr Limcano, and in the meantime, without any hesitation, the piece of chalk jumped up and wrote:

76704

Mr Limcano hastily worked out the sum on a piece of paper on his desk.

'Goodness gracious me!' he cried. 'It's quite

right! Well, that really *does* prove it, doesn't it? This is indeed a magic piece of chalk. But we must never use it up by asking simple or unnecessary questions that we should be able to answer ourselves. We must preserve it for difficult questions only.'

And that is what they have carefully done ever since. They decided not to say anything about it to the children and teachers in the other classes, not even Miss Trenham herself. They thought that with the rest of the school all joining in the questions it would use itself up in no time. Then they also decided that instead of keeping it on the ledge beneath the blackboard it would be better in a box with a lid on top. That would stop it from jumping up and wasting itself every time they asked anything, and the lid could always be removed when an answer was really needed.

And from that day to this the tiny piece of magic chalk has never failed to answer a single question, however difficult. Even on the very rare occasions when Mr Limcano has not known something himself, the chalk has been able to tell him.

So, you see, it has served two purposes.

Firstly, it has kept everybody in that class well informed.

Secondly (and even more important), the children have formed the habit of concentrating very hard on answering questions themselves without bothering the chalk. So by the time it has used itself up (and that *must* be soon, because it really is now a *very* tiddly piece of chalk) they should have developed into a very studious class indeed.

And that, Mr Limcano thinks, is probably the most magic thing in the whole story.

The statue

There it stood on a high pedestal in the market square, a large stone statue of a man with a beard. He was wearing an old-fashioned suit with a long watch chain dangling from the waistcoat pocket. I don't know if there was a stone watch on the end of the watch chain inside the pocket because I've never climbed up to look, but I doubt it. What would be the use of a stone watch anyway?

The face of that statue had a very noble expression on it. It seemed to be saying, 'All my life I never did anything wrong, and I'm proud of it.' Mind you, if the words on the pedestal were anything to go by, the statue had every reason to feel proud. This is what they said:

SIR JOSHUA POSTLETHWAITE

Born 1826. Died 28th February 1895.
Mayor of this town from 1882-1894.
Erected by his fellow citizens in gratitude for a
life of goodness, piety and devotion to duty.
Leader of Industry and Benefactor to the Poor.
Always greatly beloved by his family and
many friends.

You'd think, wouldn't you, that the people of the town would be very proud of a statue like that right in the middle of the market square, but as a matter of fact they hardly ever took any notice of it except when it caused a traffic jam, and then they thought it was a confounded nuisance. And as for Sir Joshua Postlethwaite, no one knew much about him. When strangers made inquiries about that statue, the only information they were given was that he was 'some old man who used to live here'. Who he was or what he did, no one seemed to know or care. And I'm afraid that the result was that the statue was never looked at and was no use to anybody except the starlings, who flew in from the country each night to go to sleep on Sir Joshua Postlethwaite's head, arms and shoulders and in his beard. And as you perhaps know, starlings can make an awful mess.

One Sunday afternoon Bobby Brewster happened to be in the market square when it was quite deserted, and he decided to go and look at that statue. Why he did it after all the years of ignoring the statue I don't know, but it was a jolly good thing he did, because if he hadn't I wouldn't have this story to tell.

He was reading the words on the pedestal when a very funny thing happened. A voice said, 'That's all rubbish.'

'I beg your pardon?' asked Bobby Brewster.

'I said that's all rubbish,' repeated the voice.

'What is?' asked Bobby Brewster.

'What you're reading about me,' said the voice.

'Who are you?' asked Bobby.

'I'm Sir Joshua Postlethwaite,' said the voice.

Bobby looked up in amazement, and there was the statue gazing down at him.

'Goodness gracious me! I didn't know you could talk.'

74

'As a matter of fact, I didn't know myself until just now,' said the statue. 'But there you were, the first person for months to trouble to read about me, and I felt I simply must own up. And when I opened my mouth the words simply came out. It felt very funny, I can tell you. I'm just as surprised as you are.'

'Well, now you can talk,' said Bobby, 'what do you want to say?'

'Lots,' replied Sir Joshua Postlethwaite. 'But before I tell you, I simply must change my expression. I feel such a complete fool standing here looking noble, and I'm stuck like it. Please give me time, though. It's not easy to change your expression after more than seventy years.'

Then the statue closed and opened its eyes several times and wriggled his nose and mouth about. It looked so funny grimacing that Bobby started laughing, and by the time the face on the statue settled down it was smiling too.

'That's much better,' it said.

'It is indeed,' said Bobby. 'You look quite human.'

'I am. At least, I was when I was alive,' said the

statue. 'Let's start by stopping all this Sir Joshua Postlethwaite nonsense. My friends always called me Jos, so will you please call me Jos?'

'Oh, I don't think I ought to do that,' said

Bobby. 'After all, you are a grown-up mayor with a beard, and it wouldn't be respectful. May I call you Uncle Jos? It seems to fit you.'

'If you insist,' agreed the statue.

'Good,' said Bobby. 'Now tell me, Uncle Jos, what did you mean when you said that the words on your pedestal were all rubbish?'

'Well, perhaps I was exaggerating when I said they were *all* rubbish,' said Uncle Jos. 'I *was* born in 1826 and I *did* die on the 28th February 1895, and I *was* mayor of this town for twelve years, but it's all that stuff about goodness, piety and hard work that gets my goat.'

'Why?' asked Bobby. 'It sounds very impressive to me.'

'It may sound impressive,' said Uncle Jos, 'but it's nonsense. I wasn't always good by any means. I only went to church when I felt like it and I never worked very hard. And as for always being greatly beloved by my family and friends, it simply isn't true. I often irritated my family, and some of my friends thought I was a pain in the neck.'

'And were you?' asked Bobby.

77

'Yes, I'm sure I was sometimes,' agreed Sir Joshua sadly.

'Don't worry about that, Uncle Jos,' said Bobby. 'My father sometimes says *I'm* a pain in the neck.'

'I'm sure you are,' said the statue. 'Everybody is. That's why putting me on this pedestal with that impossible description of me and making me look so noble was ridiculous. I know my fellow citizens meant it well, but what good has it done? Nobody nowadays knows or cares who I was, and nobody believes the words on the pedestal, so I'm ignored by everybody except the starlings.'

'I see what you mean,' agreed Bobby. 'Perhaps that's the result of not telling the truth about yourself.'

'*I* didn't carve the words. I was dead at the time. It isn't my fault,' protested Uncle Jos. 'It's all those silly fellow citizens.'

Then Bobby had an idea. 'You know, Uncle Jos,' he said, 'if you can talk you must be a magic statue, mustn't you?'

'Yes, I suppose I am,' agreed the statue. 'Mind

78

you, I've only just started being magic, so I'm not much good at it yet.'

'Never mind, you're sure to get better,' said Bobby soothingly, 'so why not try to be even more magic. Change the expression on your face, and see if you can alter the words to match your expression. It might be fun.'

'That's a jolly good idea,' said Uncle Jos, 'but I don't want you to look while I'm doing it because I might make a mess of it. It was painful enough changing my expression the first time. I prefer to be left alone to make my magic alterations by myself in the dark.'

'Certainly,' said Bobby. 'I must go now anyway because it's nearly tea time. I'll come and look at you again tomorrow on my way home from school.'

'Delighted to see you at any time,' said Uncle Jos. 'But don't expect me to talk to you if anyone else is here. Just because I'm a magic statue doesn't mean that I'm going to talk to any Tom, Dick or Harry. But when we are here by ourselves I don't mind talking to you because you really appreciate magic, don't you?'

'I certainly do,' agreed Bobby. And then he went home to tea.

On the following afternoon Bobby returned to look at the statue on his way home from school, and he wasn't the only one. For a change several other people were there as well. Uncle Jos was standing with a broad smile on his face, and the carving on the pedestal said:

SIR JOSHUA POSTLETHWAITE.
Born 1826. Died 28th February 1895.
Mayor of this town from 1882-1894.
Erected by his fellow citizens in memory of a friend who was nearly always cheerful and hardly ever bad-tempered.

'That's better,' thought Bobby, and other people agreed with him, because one of the onlookers said, 'What a jolly looking old man. I wonder who he was?'

Whereupon the grin on Uncle Jos's face became even broader.

And, do you know, because that statue looked so natural and the words were about an ordinary man, people showed far more interest in it. They began really to ask who Sir Joshua Postlethwaite was and what he had done when he was alive. At Bobby Brewster's school they even had a project about Sir Joshua Postlethwaite, and by borrowing books from the library they discovered that he had been a nice old man and really had tried to do good wherever he went, but he had never made a show about it when he was alive, so no wonder he objected to being made to look so noble on a statue erected by his fellow citizens.

One last funny thing happened, but only Bobby Brewster knew about it. The statue soon discovered that it became bored with keeping any expression on its face for too long. After all, even kind people don't always have a broad grin on their faces, do they? There are times when they look annoyed and there's usually a jolly good reason for it. Bobby arranged to go regularly to talk to the statue when no one else was there, and Sir Joshua took the opportunity of changing his mood. Sometimes he had a worried frown when there had been a particularly bad traffic jam. I suppose he was afraid that the autho-

rities might decide to move him because he was in the way. Sometimes he looked very annoyed when people had been throwing litter round his base, and I don't blame him. It's a pity he wasn't able to shout at them. Once during some particularly cold weather he caught a cold and sneezed several times, and that frightened the starlings so much that from that day to this they have never stood on his head, arms and shoulders and in his beard. But whenever other people were there he composed his features into the kind smile that had been so typical of him when he was

82

alive. And the result is that because the statue now looks so natural and because the words ring true, far more people look at it every day, and Sir Joshua Postlethwaite is much better known than ever he was before.

The new library

In the town where Bobby Brewster lives they have just opened a new library. At the old library he had already made great friends with the librarian, Miss Patricia Mellish, and her assistants, and he always tried to go there when they were not too busy, so that he could have a chat and ask their advice about the best books to read. Not that he always took the advice. One of the assistants – I'm not sure of her name – the pretty one – seems to like stories about moonbeams and fairies, and Bobby thinks they're silly. But after all, we can't all think alike, can we, and that made no difference to Bobby's visits. He still liked chatting to that particular assistant because she looked so nice.

However, all this has nothing to do with my story, which is supposed to be about the new library. At long last, with a most impressive ceremony at which several important people made speeches – some of them too long – it was opened about a month ago. At first, after the old small room where everyone got in everyone else's way, the new building seemed almost too grand, but Bobby soon got used to it, especially as it has a special children's room, not only for keeping books, but for reading them as well. He has found this most useful, because he can look through books before taking them away and make sure that they are about more sensible things than fairies and moonbeams.

For a week or so after the opening, the new library always seemed to be full of people staring around, but things soon settled down and this story is about a funny thing that happened to Bobby Brewster when he was all by himself one Tuesday afternoon looking through the shelves of children's books. He had chosen a book to look at when a voice said:

'What about me?'

'I beg your pardon?' asked Bobby Brewster.

'I said what about me?' repeated the voice.

85

Well, no one else was there, so Bobby could hardly answer what about it when he didn't even know whose voice it was, could he?

'Who are you?' he asked.

'I'm in the red book on the bottom shelf,' said the voice.

Bobby put back the book he was holding and looked along the bottom shelf, which had lots of red books on it. He picked one up.

'No, not that one,' said the voice. 'More to your left.'

Bobby tried another one.

'No! No!' cried the voice. 'A larger book than that.'

'This one?' asked Bobby, picking out the largest red book he could find.

'No, that's *too* large,' cried the voice, and it sounded quite annoyed.

'Don't fluster me,' said Bobby. 'It's surprising enough to hear you talking at all without all that shouting. I'll tell you what I'll do. I'll touch every red book on the shelf and when I come to you just say "Yes".'

So that's what he did, and in a very short time

he touched a medium-sized red book and the voice said 'Yes'.

Bobby took the book from the shelf and looked at it. It was called *The Adventures of Tommy*.

'Well,' he said, 'it *looks* an ordinary enough book to me.'

'Turn to page 22,' said the voice.

Bobby did as he was told, but it was just a

printed page in the middle of the book with no pictures on it.

'Now turn to page 69,' said the voice.

On page 69 there was a picture of a donkey.

'Are you a donkey?' asked Bobby.

'Don't be rude,' said the voice. 'Turn back to page 9.'

'It's all very well talking about not being rude,' said Bobby, 'but why didn't you ask me to turn to page 9 in the first place?'

'Because I wanted to be sure you were clever enough to read your figures,' said the voice.

By this time Bobby had found page 9 and on it there was a picture of a cheerful-looking boy. And as Bobby looked at the picture, a very funny thing happened. The boy stepped straight out of the page and on to the table. He did, really. Then he said:

'Now you've found me at last. My name's Tommy. What's yours?'

'I'm Bobby Brewster,' said Bobby Brewster.

'How do you do?' said Tommy, and they shook hands.

'Well,' said Bobby, 'this is the most amazing

thing. I've had some extraordinary adventures in my time, but never anything like this before. Are you a *real* boy?'

'Not exactly,' said Tommy, 'but I'm a book boy, which is just as good.'

'What do you mean by a book boy?' asked Bobby.

'All the people in books are book people,' said Tommy.

'Are they really?' asked Bobby. 'And can they all walk about and talk as you do?'

'Certainly they can,' said Tommy. 'Only they usually do it at nights when the library's closed. It would never do if all the book people started crowding out the library and getting mixed up with the ordinary people who had come to borrow books, would it?'

'No, I suppose not,' agreed Bobby. 'And anyway, they wouldn't want to borrow books about themselves, would they? But if they only come out at nights, what are you doing here in the middle of the afternoon?'

'I felt I simply must talk to you,' said Tommy, 'and as there are so few people about, it seemed a good opportunity to ask you to do me a favour.'

'What would you like?' asked Bobby.

'Will you *please* borrow me from the library?' asked Tommy. 'You see, I'm not in a very well-known book, and since I was put into stock when the new library opened, not a single person has borrowed me. So I've been stuck up on the shelf day after day, and, let me tell you, it's jolly boring.'

'It must be,' agreed Bobby Brewster. 'Very well, Tommy. I *will* borrow you – on one condition. Will you promise me that none of your adventures is about fairies or moonbeams?'

'Of course I will,' said Tommy contemptuously. 'Who ever *wants* adventures with fairies and moonbeams?'

'The pretty librarian over there does for one,' said Bobby.

'She must be mad even if she is pretty,' said Tommy. 'Come on now, you promised you'd borrow me and I can't wait to get out of the library and home with you.'

Bobby took *The Adventures of Tommy* over

to the desk and it was stamped by the pretty librarian.

'I hope you enjoy this book, Bobby,' she said.

'I have an idea that it's going to be the most exciting book I've ever read,' said Bobby Brewster.

It was. Bobby saved up *The Adventures of Tommy* to read every evening when he went to bed. And Tommy wasn't just a boy in a book.

He seemed like a real boy. As soon as Bobby opened the book at page 9 Tommy jumped out on to the bedside table, and as Bobby read his adventures he could actually *see* Tommy having them. It is difficult for me to explain, but all I can say is this: Bobby had *never* felt so excited when reading a book before, and he thought to himself that if all book people were like that, he'd have to read and read and read and never stop borrowing books from the new library.

But all good things come to an end. By the weekend Bobby had read the last of Tommy's adventures, and he closed the book and put it down with a sigh. Then a voice said:

'Turn to page 9.'

Bobby did as he was told, and Tommy jumped out on to the bedside table. 'Did you enjoy my adventures?' he asked.

'They were grand,' said Bobby. 'And do you know what I'm going to do? I'm going to tell all my friends about you so *The Adventures of Tommy* won't be stuck on the library shelves any more, because they'll all want to borrow you.'

'That's very good of you,' said Tommy. 'There's nothing like a change. But, as a matter of fact, I shall be quite glad to get back to the library for a time so that I can meet my book friends in the evenings again.'

'What do you actually do at nights?' asked Bobby.

'Oh, we talk together and play games, and swing up and down the library curtains and have a grand old time,' said Tommy. 'I've met *lots* of nice people like Mary Poppins and Toad of Toad Hall. Not that they're all nice by any means. I expect you have read about some horrid people in books, haven't you?'

'Indeed I have,' agreed Bobby. 'People like the Ugly Sisters in *Cinderella*.'

'Well, they're just as horrid in the library at nights as they are in the books,' said Tommy. 'But the book policemen keep them in order, so they don't bother us all that much and nobody ever takes any notice of them.'

'It would be lovely to meet them all,' said Bobby Brewster.

'Oh, you can *meet* them easily enough by just

borrowing the books and reading about them,' said Tommy, 'but if you actually want to see them and *talk* to them all together, *you'll* have to get someone to write a book about you and put it in the library shelves. Then *you'll* be a book boy and be able to have fun with the book people in the library at nights.'

When Bobby took *The Adventures of Tommy* back to the library the next day he was in a thoughtful mood. Miss Patricia Mellish herself was at the counter.

'Miss Mellish,' asked Bobby, 'when you come into the library the first thing in the morning, does it ever look as if little people have been running about and having games during the night?'

'Well, I can't say that,' said Miss Mellish, 'because by the time I get here the place has been polished and cleaned. But I have noticed *one* funny thing. Although I pull the curtains carefully every evening before closing, in the morning they always look untidy as if little people have been swinging on them. I wonder why?'

Bobby said nothing, but kept his thoughts to himself. And that afternoon, when he got home from the library with a new book, *I* happened to be at the Brewsters' house. You know who I am, don't you? H. E. Todd. I've known Bobby all his life and he always tells me about his extraordinary adventures.

'Hullo, Bobby,' I asked. 'Has anything funny happened to you recently?'

'Yes,' said Bobby Brewster, 'as a matter of fact

it has.' And he told me all about *The Adventures of Tommy* and the book people in the library.

'Do you know,' I said. 'That'll make a story for me to write. I'll put it in a book with some other stories about you, and then if I can persuade the librarian to buy the book, you *will* be on the library shelves, and you *will* be able to talk to all your book friends at nights.'

So that's exactly what I did – and here's the story I wrote.

And I hope you've enjoyed reading it.